Anything is possible!

by Jennifer Armstrong

Illustrated by Peggy Lipschutz

Library of Congress Catalog Card Number 2006936586
ISBN 978-0-9769827-1-5

A production of:
  Wren Song Press
  233 Poors Mill Road
  Belfast, Maine 04915
  207-338-6616
  www.jenniferarmstrong.com

WREN SONG
P R E S S

Graphic Design by Al Trescot, Rocky Hill Design, Damariscotta, Maine
Printed in U.S.A. by J.S. McCarthy, Augusta, Maine

I love getting up in the morning

I jump out of bed

as soon as   I wake up

and do   a few cartwheels

When Mama says,
"Time to get dressed, Sylvie"

I stand in front of
the closet

put my hand on
the door

and take a
deep breath

That's the best part!

*Before I decide
what to wear*

Anything is possible!

Sometimes I wear all stripes

Sometimes I wear a
tu-tu on my head

Sometimes I wear red
from hat
to shoes

You just never know
what you might look like

I love going to our mailbox

I run out the door

as fast as I can go

When Mama says,

"Sylvie, you can
check the mail"

I stand on my tiptoes

close my eyes

and take a deep breath

That's the best part!

Right before I put my hand in the mailbox

Anything is possible!

Slowly
I reach inside and
pull out

letters

postcards

magazines

a spray of lilac

a purple shell

You never know what good surprises might be there

Anything is possible!

I love my Mama's stories

I race over to her and climb
up on her lap when she says,

"Sylvie, it's storytime"

I snuggle up against her
close my eyes
and take a deep breath

That's the best part!

Right before Mama says, "Once upon a time …"

Anything is possible!

Sometimes Mama tells me
about when she was little

or when I was little

And sometimes she makes up stories

Mama skating on a frozen pond

A tree growing gold and silver apples

Me eating my first chocolate cake

You just never know what
wonderful pictures you'll
see in your mind

Anything
is possible

I love to draw

When Mama says, "Sylvie, I bought you a new pad of paper"

I race for
my crayons
and pencils

I spread out that
   new, clean, empty sheet of paper
      as fast as I can

I pick out a color
   hold it high above the paper
      and take a deep breath

That's the best part!

Right before I make a mark on the page

Anything is possible!

Sometimes I draw people or places I know

Sometimes I make up animals and flowers

I love Mama singing me to sleep

I dash up the stairs
when Mama says,
"Bedtime, Sylvie"

I brush my teeth
make faces in the mirror

throw off my shoes
with a spin
and a kick

I hug my stuffed tiger
burrow into the blankets
and take a deep breath
That's the best part!

Right before Mama starts singing

Anything is possible!

Sometimes Mama sings silly songs

Sometimes Mama sings quiet songs

and sometimes we make up songs about ME!

Anything Is Possible

Based on a song collected by Ruth Crawford Seeger
and folk-processed by Gerry Armstrong and Jennifer Armstrong

Syl - vie wore a red shirt, a red shirt, a red shirt,
Syl - vie did some cart - wheels, cart - wheels cart - wheels,

Syl - vie wore a red shirt all day long. Oh yes,
Syl - vie did some cart - wheels when she got up.

Syl - vie had a good— day, Oh yes, Syl - vie had a good— day, Oh yes,

Syl - vie had a good— day, For an - y - thing is pos - si - ble.

Sylvie checked the mail box, the mail box, the mail box
Sylvie checked the mail box and found a shell

Sylvie made up stories, stories, stories
Sylvie made up stories of kings and crowns

Sylvie drew a picture, a picture, a picture
Sylvie drew a picture of a rainbow bird

Sylvie drew a deep breath, a deep breath, a deep breath
Sylvie drew a deep breath and fell asleep.

Try singing your child's name in this song. Have fun with it.

Jennifer Armstrong is a musical
storyteller and shares songs and stories
with audiences of all ages across the
country. Her programs, recordings, books
and pies, encourage the creative artist
inside each of us.

Thank you Peggy for your fabulous drawings.
Thank you Meg, Meredith and Pippi for your
love and encouragement.

Thank you to my mother, Gerry Armstrong, for
telling me bedtime stories and making up
songs about me.

Peggy Lipschutz is a graduate of Pratt Institute in
Brooklyn, N.Y. She is an English-born painter, illustrator
and cartoonist, known widely for her "Chalk Talks"

Peggy is delighted to be working with Jennifer Armstrong,
an artist she has long admired for her humor, her
music, her stories and her Peach pie.

"With irrepressible optimism and glee, Jennifer Armstrong shows us how, in every moment of our daily lives, truly Anything is Possible."

Molly Bang
children's author and illustrator

This lovely read aloud bedtime story, from musical storyteller Jennifer Armstrong, is full of breathing room and gives space for happiness in ordinary, every day pleasures.

The loose sketches, full of vigor and joy, from illustrator Peggy Lipschutz are the perfect compliment to the story.

This book is for children ages 2 to 8 and is designed wide so it is easy to hold a child on your lap while reading.

For older readers, ages 6 to 12, look for Jennifer's first book, *The Poet's Basket*. It too is a story that celebrates creative possibilities.

ISBN-13: 978-0-9769827-1-5
ISBN-10: 0-9769827-1-4